EMMA JUST MEDIUM: The Friend Dilemma

Laura Wiltse Prior

with illustrations by Marta Kissi

Egremont, Massachusetts

One Elm Books is an imprint of Red Chair Press LLC
Red Chair Press LLC PO Box 333 South Egremont, MA 01258-0333
www.redchairpress.com
Free Discussion Guide available online.

For Mom and Dad who were there for me through my own dilemmas.
—Laura

Names: Prior, Laura Wiltse, author. | Kissi, Marta, illustrator.

Title: Emma Just Medium. The friend dilemma / Laura Wiltse Prior ; with illustrations by Marta Kissi.

Other titles: Friend dilemma

Description: Egremont, Massachusetts : One Elm Books, an imprint of Red Chair Press, [2025] | Series: Emma Just Medium ; [2] | Interest age level: 007-010. | Summary: Emma's topsy-turvy summer led her to eagerly anticipate reuniting with friends Lily and Amelia for familiar activities. However, when they meet before second grade begins, unexpected changes occur: Lily becomes a ballerina, Amelia loses interest in science, and they both enjoy hanging out with Emma's younger brother Little. Determined to restore their bond, Emma tries to impress them during the school bus ride. Yet, second grade unfolds with more differences than expected.--Publisher.

Identifiers: ISBN: 978-1-947159-82-2 (hardcover) | 978-1-947159-83-9 (ebook PDF) | 978-1-947159-84-6 (ePub3 S&L) | 978-1-947159-85-3 (ePub3 TR) | 978-1-947159-86-0 (ebook Kf8) | 978-1-947159-94-5 (audiobook) | LCCN: 2024933220

Subjects: LCSH: Middle-born children--Juvenile fiction. | Siblings--Juvenile fiction. | Friendship-- Juvenile fiction. | Change--Juvenile fiction. | Adaptability (Psychology)--Juvenile fiction. | Interpersonal communication--Juvenile fiction. | CYAC: Middle-born children--Fiction. | Siblings--Fiction. | Friendship--Fiction. | Change--Fiction. | Adaptability--Fiction. | Interpersonal communication--Fiction. | BISAC: JUVENILE FICTION / Social Themes / Self-Esteem & Self-Reliance. | JUVENILE FICTION / Social Themes / Friendship. | JUVENILE FICTION / Family / Siblings.

Classification: LCC: PZ7.1.P768 Emf 2025 | DDC: [E]--dc23

LC record available at https://lccn.loc.gov/2024933220
Main body text set in Baskerville 16/23
Text copyright Laura Wiltse Prior
Copyright © 2025 Red Chair Press LLC

RED CHAIR PRESS, ONE ELM Books logo, and green leaf colophon are registered trademarks of Red Chair Press LLC.

All rights reserved. No part of this book may be reproduced, stored in an information or retrieval system, or transmitted in any form by any means, electronic, mechanical including photocopying, recording, or otherwise without the prior written permission from the Publisher. For permissions, contact info@redchairpress.com

Printed in the United States of America

0924 1P S25CG

Table of Contents

Chapter 1   Playdate Plans................1

Chapter 2   Dinner Plans................18

Chapter 3   The Bus Plan 22

Chapter 4   Lunch Plans 35

Chapter 5   The New Playdate Plan 44

Chapter 6   Big's Plans................54

Chapter 7   Little's Plan................58

Chapter 8   The Playground Plan 64

Chapter 9   Sprained But Not Broken 73

Chapter 10   Let's Start The Show 77

CHAPTER 1
Playdate Plans

Emma couldn't wait. She had the whole playdate planned to the minute. First, Lego® creations. Then, science experiments. And last, soccer. These were the Special Friend Crew's favorites and Emma loved to plan them for all their playdates. Emma wanted this playdate to be extra special because she hadn't seen Lily and Amelia since her beach vacation—one whole month. It felt like infinity. And Emma had just found out that this year the girls wouldn't be in the same class together like last year. She had to make sure the Special Friend Crew was as special and crewish as ever for third grade.

Emma went to her room to get the giant magical Lego dragon she'd been working on all week. Lily loved Legos and Amelia loved dragons. This combination would make them both happy. Emma carried the creature down the stairs, careful not to crush its delicate wings. It was so tall she couldn't see over the top. She made it to the bottom step when her sock slipped. Emma fell backward. The dragon flew into the air. For a second, it looked like a real flying dragon. Then BOOM! it hit the floor. Its head slid towards the couch; his body scattered over the family room carpet.

"Good one," said Big, her older brother, relaxing on the couch. He was acting like he could really drive even though he was just playing a video game and he was only twelve. Emma's younger brother, Little, sat on the floor in front of Big, steering an imaginary wheel.

"I can drive, too," he said with a *w* in drive instead of an *r*.

"Yeah, you're fast," Big said, eyes glued to the screen.

Emma sat up and rubbed her back where she fell. She gathered as many Legos as she could in her arms and tried to carry them to the table. They fell like raindrops as she went, making a long trail. She'd never be able to rebuild the dragon in time. Especially because she could barely see with the tears welling up in her eyes.

"Can you guys help me? My Special Friend Crew is coming and we're doing dragon Legos and powerful potions and then soccer. It'll take a million years to pick all this up." The boys looked at each other. Big grinned. Little smiled back at him. Emma held her breath.

"No way," Big said.

"No way, Emma Bemma. We're driving," Little said, laughing. He climbed onto the couch next to Big and put his thumb in his mouth. Emma Just Medium – again, the yucky way she felt when it seemed like she didn't matter very much, sandwiched between her two brothers. She kicked at the Legos. It stung her toes.

Then the doorbell rang. Emma leapt over the mess. She sprinted to the door and pulled it open. Lily stood there in front of her dad.

"Emma!" said Lily.

"You're here!" said Emma. Suddenly the destroyed dragon didn't matter at all. She hugged her friend. She had missed her even more than she thought. Then she pulled back. She took in what Lily was wearing—a pink tutu, a high bun in her hair, and a crown.

"Why are you wearing that?" Emma asked. Mommy appeared behind Emma just then, putting her hands on her shoulders and giving them a little squeeze. That was Mommy language for *don't be rude.*

"Lily," Mommy sang, "How great to see you."

"I'm a ballerina," answered Lily. She bent her knees sideways and dipped down low, holding her hands wide. She put her lips together like she was going to kiss someone.

"This is a plié," she said.

"She took classes over the summer and now she can't get enough," Lily's dad said, smiling.

"Wonderful," said Mommy. Emma wasn't so sure about that.

"Well, have fun, girls. See you in a few hours," Lily's dad said, returning to his car. Emma decided to forget about the plié thing and kissing face.

"Let's build," Emma said. She grabbed Lily's hand and led her to the Lego land on the floor.

"Lily, Lily!" exclaimed Little. He was always excited to see Emma's friends. But he got in the way of her plans a lot.

"Don't bother us, Little," Emma started to warn, but then she switched to the gentler voice that she learned to use with him a few summers ago. "Let us play alone a little while, okay?"

"Aww, he's so cute," said Lily. "He can play with us." Emma pursed her lips.

"I already put the Legos out," she told Lily, gesturing at the floor. Then she sat down on the carpet.

Lily didn't sit. Emma looked up at her.

"Why are you standing like that?" Emma asked.

"This is first position," said Lily.

"Why do you need a position?"

"It's for ballet. I have to practice. This is second." She stepped one foot outward and stood like a duck. Emma didn't know what to say.

"Want to know third?" asked Lily. Emma didn't.

She just wanted to get started on the plan. Ballet was not part of it and never had been.

She was happy that the doorbell rang just then.

"Amelia," she cheered. Amelia would be excited about Emma's plans.

"Ameela!" Little echoed. Mommy answered the door. Amelia stepped in. Her hair was still long and shiny, down to her waist. She wore blue leggings and a big purple t-shirt. She looked just like Amelia. No bun, no tutu—phew.

"Let's do our Special Friend Crew move!" Emma said. The girls got in a circle, clapped their hands together three times and jumped up to high five on each side. Emma's right hand whooshed through the air, missing Amelia's.

WHACK

Lily's hand missed Emma's and hit her face.

"Are you ok?" Lily asked Emma. Emma nodded even though her face burned. They were out of practice.

"Let's build a Lego dragon," said Emma. "I know just what we need to do."

"Dragons are kind of… boring," said Amelia. Emma's stomach dropped. How were flying and fire-breathing mythical beasts boring?

"That's okay," she said, even though it wasn't. "We could make a monster. Or build an airplane. Or a really tall tower, or…"

"We're third-graders now, so…" Amelia said. Emma wasn't sure what that meant.

"I have an idea!" Lily raised her finger into the air like she always did when she had a good one. Maybe she had a great Lego plan.

"Let's play ballet class," Lily said.

Emma's stomach clenched. Ballet class? That wasn't a good idea at all.

Lily continued, "I'll be the teacher, Ms. Vanderbilt, and you'll be my students. Amelia, you'll be the best one in class and Emma is the naughty kid," Lily said.

Emma stood up straight. "Why am I the bad one?" she asked.

Lily shrugged, "Someone has to get in trouble." Emma tried to hold back her anger, but she felt like a monster was fighting to come out.

"See? You're being naughty right now," pointed out Amelia.

"Let's practice pirouettes," said Ms. 'Lily' Vanderbilt. Lily twirled on one foot, with her hands in front of her like she was holding a bowl of eggs. Amelia copied her. Emma stood like her feet were stuck in cement.

"Pirette!" said Little. He started spinning in circles on two feet. He stumbled and fell into Emma. Little was very bad at ballet. Emma could do better if she ever wanted to try. But she definitely did not want to.

"Well done, Little," said Ms. Vanderbilt.

"But…"

"Ms. Emma, no talking in the middle of class. Please go sit in the corner."

"But I…"

"No cookies for you at snack time if you say one more word."

Emma opened her mouth, then shut it. Mommy usually gave them carrot sticks and crackers with seeds that stuck in their teeth. What if Ms. Vanderbilt really had cookies?

Emma stomped away. She stepped hard on a Lego. Her foot hurt and so did her brain from this playdate. She hopped the rest of the way. She wasn't excited anymore. She was back to Emma Just Medium—no, now she was Emma the Naughty Kid.

Just then, Spiky dashed in from his walk with Dad. He wagged his fuzzy tail when he saw Emma in the corner.

"Here, Spiky!" Emma called. Spiky always came when she called. He started to run over to Emma. Then he spotted the Legos. He chomped a big mouthful.

"Drop it!" yelled Emma. Spiky spit them out in a slobbery pile. Then he ran over to join ballet class. The teacher told him he was very good at the jumps even though he looked clumsy. Emma sucked in her breath as hard as she could so no tears would sneak out.

After a million years, Ms. Vanderbilt said it was

break time. Finally. Now they could do something fun.

"I'll get my Powerful Potions book!" Emma shouted, running to the bookshelf. She grabbed the heavy book and put it on the kitchen table. It was a special present her Grandpa gave her, filled with cool experiments you could do in your own house. One day in second grade, the Special Friend Crew mixed milk with soap and food coloring and made shimmery rainbows. Another time they made bouncy balls. And one time they made raisins dance. Experiment time was Emma's favorite part of their playdates.

The girls thumbed through the pictures. Emma pointed out a photo of homemade slime. Amelia looked at Lily and grimaced.

"Too sticky," said Amelia.

"Yeah nasty," said Lily.

"What about these melted crayons?" Emma asked.

"Boring," said Amelia. Lily nodded.

"A tornado in a bottle?" Amelia made a face like she smelled dirty socks. So did Lily.

"A balloon race? A lava lamp? Dancing raisins?" Emma tried.

"Not again," said Amelia.

"Nope," said Lily.

"I know!" Emma said, "We could make Galaxy in a Jar!" No one could say no to Galaxy in a Jar. The other girls looked at each other. Emma held her breath. Then they shook their heads together at the same time. Emma's shoulders sank.

Lily rose up on her tippy toes. Amelia did the same. Ballet class was back in session. Emma slammed the book shut as hard as she could. The girls fell back onto flat feet. They stared at Emma. Her face felt like it was on fire.

"All okay in here?" called Mommy, stepping into the kitchen.

"I don't like experiments anymore," Emma said, crossing her arms over her chest.

"But you love science," said Mommy, raising her eyebrows. She looked at each of the girls' faces, then said, "Maybe not today. Can you find something else to play? Emma, didn't you set up the soccer goals?"

"That sounds fun," Lily said.

"Yeah, let's play soccer," said Amelia. Emma thought about it. She did love soccer. They all did. But the Special Friend Crew playdate was already ruined. Soccer wasn't going to fix it.

"Soccer is… boring," Emma said.

Lily's finger went up in the air again. "I have an idea! Let's pretend Little's a baby and we are his babysitters!" she said. But Little was already Emma's baby brother in real life.

Little ran over. He lay on the floor and said, "Goo goo ga ga." He sucked his thumb. The girls wrapped him up in the blanket from the couch. They talked about how cute he was. They pretended to give him a bottle. Emma just stood there. The girls didn't notice. She wished she could get in a time machine like the one in her favorite book and fly back to second grade when they all played Legos, made potions, and played soccer. Just like Emma planned.

She looked around. Big was still playing his video game. Emma sat next to him on the couch.

"Can I play?"

"What about the special soccer potions and powerful crew dragons and all that?" Big asked, rolling his eyes.

She didn't bother to correct him. She glanced over at Amelia, Lily, and Little, a new trio. Then she looked at the dragon she'd kicked in pieces on the floor. Last year everything would have gone according to plan. This wasn't a good sign for third grade.

"They're all broken," she said. She swallowed a lump in her throat. Then she held up her hands and steered an imaginary wheel away from that playdate.

CHAPTER 2
Dinner Plans

The night before the first day of school, Daddy brought home pizza. Big took huge bites of his slice and chewed with his mouth open like a washing machine. Little dropped bits on the floor for Spiky when he thought no one was looking. Emma nibbled at her slice like a mouse.

"Emma, what's wrong? You love pizza," said Dad.

"It's boring," Emma said. Maybe that's how third-graders were supposed to sound. Mommy and Dad looked at each other.

"Maybe your tastes are maturing. Do you want to try our dinner?" Mommy asked. Emma looked at Mommy's plate. It was pink slimy fish. Emma thought of Special, Star, and Silly who were swimming around in their bowls in her room.

"I don't eat sea creatures," said Emma. "They're my friends." Mommy made a face like her salmon didn't taste so good anymore.

"Did something happen with your human friends today?" asked Dad.

"They're my friends!" Little said, pointing to himself.

"No, Little, they're not your friends, they're…" Emma started to correct her brother. Then she stopped. Was he right? Lily and Amelia didn't like to do what she did anymore. And now they probably didn't even like *her* anymore since she wouldn't play ballet, or babysitter, or even soccer. When her friends had left the playdate the other day, Mommy made Emma come to the door and say goodbye even though she didn't want to. Lily and Amelia had both given her a strange look. Emma's pulse sped up thinking of it. They were probably kicking her out of the Special Friend Crew. Maybe that was goodbye forever.

"I'm sure things will be better at school," said Mommy. But Amelia and Lily wouldn't even be in her class. How would she be able to fix things? In life without her Special Friend Crew everything would be different, a bad different. She wouldn't have a special move, she wouldn't have a lunch bunch, and she wouldn't have a recess group. She had to stay part of the crew or third grade would never be as good as second. Emma thought and thought. Maybe she could change things back to how they were before. But how?

* * *

When Emma pulled down her covers to get into bed that night, she noticed it was the sheet with the purple star in the top corner, the spot Mommy called a stain. It was from the time the Special Friend Crew made slime from the Powerful Potion book. They added glitter and food coloring and called it Super Crew Goo. It smelled and stuck to your fingers. They loved it. Emma had placed the Super Crew

Goo on her bed when she went to sleep that night. In the morning, she had a permanent reminder of their experiment on her sheet. The spot annoyed Mommy but usually made Emma smile. Not tonight. Now it looked like a stain to Emma too. She covered it up with a pillow and tried to block out her bad day.

Emma lay on top of the spot for a long time. She couldn't sleep. Lily and Amelia used to like everything Emma planned. They never made a change and always had fun. Now, she felt like she was at the edge of a cliff that was crumbling under her feet. She was about to fall way down to a terrible third-grade year. She wished she could fix everything with a magic wand.

That was it! The idea came to her. She would take action tomorrow. Hopefully, by tomorrow night, the stain would be a Super Crew Goo star again.

CHAPTER 3

Emma woke up extra early on the first day of third grade. Her insides did a backflip. Time to get to work.

First, she had to say her "Good morning," to her three fighting-fish, Special, Star, and Sunshine. They each had their own separate tank so they wouldn't hurt each other. Star and Special were swimming in circles in the same direction, but Sunshine was out of sync, going the other way.

"I understand," Emma whispered.

Then she went down to the kitchen before everyone else woke up and put her plan into action.

When she heard Mommy's footsteps on the stairs a half hour later, Emma scurried to sit at the kitchen counter.

"You're up early. You must be excited for the big day," Mommy said when she walked in.

"I feel like fish are swimming around in my tummy, even though I didn't eat any of the salmon last night," Emma said.

"Hmm, maybe a little nervous? Sometimes nerves and excitement blend all together." That made sense to Emma but it wasn't school she was all mixed up about, it was the Special Friend Crew.

"Remember a new year can bring change," Mommy continued. "Speaking of change, would you like to change into a special outfit for the first day?" Emma looked down at her Creature Cruise t-shirt from their beach vacation and her favorite green shorts.

"I'm already wearing something special," she said.

"I know you love that outfit, but you wore it all summer. How about something different?"

"I don't like different," Emma said.

"Sometimes people change their minds," Mommy said.

"Not me," said Emma. But she knew Mommy was right. Some people did change. Would they change back?

Mommy squinted, looking closely at Emma. "What's that white stuff on your face, honey?" she asked. Emma tried to swipe away the evidence of what she'd been doing that morning but Mommy took a tissue from her bathrobe. She seemed to have a magical pouch in there with everything including hair bands, safety pins, and wipes. She wet the tissue under the sink and came towards Emma. Emma ducked but Mommy was too much of a parent expert to miss. She smeared the tissue over Emma's face as Emma squirmed, her feet flailing around.

"Ouch," said a voice, "You kicked me!"

Emma jumped. "Little, I didn't know you were there!"

"I was hiding," Little said, popping out from under

the counter, his chin tilted up proudly.

"How long have you been there?" Emma asked.

"A loooong time," he said. Emma's stomach squeezed. Had he seen what she was up to that morning?

Mommy started to unload the dishwasher, putting items into cabinets and drawers. Emma hoped Mommy didn't notice something was missing.

Once Big, Dad and Spiky came downstairs, Dad made his famous chocolate chip waffles. Emma could only eat three, not five like usual. What if her plan didn't work?

Then Dad sang, "Let's go, let's go, let's start the show." That meant it was time for the bus stop. The whole family walked down, Spiky on his leash. As the bus drove towards them, Mommy kissed Emma's cheek and hugged her tight.

"Take deep breaths when you get that funny feeling in your stomach and you'll feel better," she said. Then Mommy pulled back and made a funny face. She brought her nose to Emma's backpack and sniffed.

"Honey, what's that smell?" Emma held her breath. Mommy was going to look in her backpack and ruin her plan.

"The bus!" Little interrupted, jumping up and down.

"The bus!" Emma echoed. Everyone turned to look at the bus moving towards them. Phew.

Dad whispered, "Go get 'em, Em," in her ear, his special saying just for Emma.

When the bus doors opened, Little tried to run up the stairs. Spiky pulled after him. Dad had to grab both of them. Little started to cry. Last summer, when Emma wanted to be older, younger, or anything other than Just Medium, she wound up learning that it was good to enjoy the stage you were at. Little hadn't learned that lesson yet.

"You'll take the bus when you're older," Emma said, bending down to him. "Have fun at pre-K for now."

Emma climbed the bus steps behind Big. A familiar smell of sneakers and bananas hit her nose. Big zipped to the very back where the fifth-graders sat and plopped down. Emma bit her lip. She scanned the seats. She remembered the first day of kindergarten when she didn't know where to sit and burst out crying in front of the entire bus. But back then when she finally got to row six, someone had said, "Want to sit with me?" That's how Emma had met Lily. They sat together every day of kindergarten and first grade. Then Amelia joined them in second grade. The Special Friend Crew sat there every bus ride since. Emma thought they would stay there together in third, fourth and fifth grade. Maybe all the way until college. But that wouldn't happen if they weren't friends anymore. Emma had to fix that. She opened her backpack and carefully removed the container she took from Mommy's Tupperware drawer that morning. Emma winced. Only some of the liquid was left. A lot had spilled in her backpack. Hopefully she had enough.

"Go on now," the new bus driver said. What happened to smiley Sid, her second-grade driver? He gave out lollipops with chocolate in the middle and told silly jokes. Everything was changing.

Emma began to walk, holding the container of liquid carefully. She swung her head side to side, looking for Lily. Two new kindergarteners huddled in row one, giggling. Another hugged herself across the way, looking out the window. Sara Coprio was combing her hair in row three next to Justin Leonard who picked at his ears. Row four was empty, and row five was packed with lots of kids Emma didn't know kicking each other. Where was Lily? Was she in row six like usual? Then Emma would be able to show her the special surprise and things could go right back to normal. Finally she got to row six.

A boy with curly hair was in Lily's place!

"Sit down back there," commanded the driver. But she couldn't yet. She had to find Lily.

LURCH. The bus was moving. What was this driver doing? Sid never drove until everyone was seated. OOPS! Emma lost her balance. She shifted right, then left, grabbing a seat back with one hand. Liquid sloshed from the container onto her Creature Cruise shirt. She stepped forward, unbalanced.

"Sit!"

SQUEAK. The bus brakes squealed. Emma tumbled forward into the seat two rows ahead. Her backpack smacked her in the back of the head. Green liquid spilled everywhere, including the lap of the person sitting there. Lily!

Emma scrambled to stand up.

"Why are you in row eight?" Emma asked Lily.

"I... I'm all wet!" cried Lily, wiping at her lap.

"It's the special..." Emma started to explain what she brought. But Lily screeched, "Eww! It's all over my new skirt!" She crinkled her nose. It reminded her of how Lily had looked at the Powerful Potion book yesterday.

"Sorry. I was just trying… I was… forget it, it was a stupid idea," Emma said. Suddenly her great plan didn't seem great anymore.

"Take a seat!," called the driver. Emma did not like him. She didn't like this bus or anyone on it. Faces peeked out from the rows, some with wide eyes, some laughing. Emma was hot. Her mouth was dry. She wanted to leave. She wanted to rewind to before the bad playdate. Or better yet, go back to second grade. But she was stuck on the bus. And Lily liked her less than ever. All she could do was go to the back, as far away as possible. She dragged her legs down the extra-long bus aisle. The whole bus stared at her. On to row nine, row ten. Emma had never been this far back.

"Can I sit with you?" she asked Big with relief when she found him in row eleven. But he gestured to

Jeremy in the spot next to him. Jeremy was throwing grapes in the air, trying to catch them in his mouth. They were missing his face and landing on the floor.

"Why are you all wet?" Big asked.

Emma shrugged. If she answered, she might cry. That would be as embarrassing as kindergarten. A grape bounced off Emma's head. She crushed it under her shoe and kept walking. She sat down next to a girl with a ponytail and a yellow dress. The girl sneered. "Fifth-graders only." Her braces had black stuff stuck in them.

Emma jumped up. She moved to the mini seat in the very back by herself. She slumped so no one could see her. She tried to take the deep breaths Mommy reminded her about. They got stuck in her throat.

The bus screeched to a stop. Amelia climbed on. Emma's heart squeezed when she saw her hair. It was wrapped up tight in a high bun, just like Lily's.

Now they were both ballerinas. Amelia got on her tippy toes and looked around. A hand raised up and waved. Amelia walked to row eight and dropped into the seat next to Lily. Emma's stomach dropped at the same time.

The container Emma took from the kitchen was almost empty now. The magical best friend potion

she invented wasn't winning her friends back. Instead, it was all over the bus floor, on her Creature Cruise shirt and worst of all, on Lily's lap. She put the container on the seat next to her. She would pretend she didn't know where it came from.

It was strange back there at the back of the bus, looking at the back of everyone's heads. Especially the two heads with the buns.

CHAPTER 4
Lunch Plans

Even though they weren't in her class like last year, Lily and Amelia were all Emma could think about. She couldn't focus on what her new teacher was saying. Ms. Smeltzer sneezed a lot and squinted even though she wore big, round glasses. She didn't hand out pencils with fun erasers like Mr. Cooper did on the first day of second grade. Emma missed Mr. Cooper. She missed every single thing from last year.

At snack time, Emma pulled out the paper bag she'd packed that morning. Instead of finding crunchy goldfish, she got a handful of wet mush. The best friend potion didn't go well with crackers. It didn't go well on anything. Emma threw the bag in the garbage and watched the other kids eat their snacks as her stomach rumbled.

Spanish was next. In first and second grade, Emma loved Spanish. Not anymore. They didn't sing fun songs this year. Or learn animal names. They talked about the weather. It was *abarrido*, which meant boring, which she learned in second grade when Spanish used to be *divertido*, which meant fun.

Later, when Ms. Smeltzer announced a school-wide group science project, Emma's chest rose for a second. Then it sank quickly like syrup in water in one of her potions. A science project wouldn't be fun without her Special Friend Crew.

In writing period, Emma wasn't allowed to create stories about magical sea creatures like last year. Instead, she had to write a "slice of life." Emma's slice of life felt like burnt pizza with slimy spinach on top.

By the time the lunch bell rang, Emma's guts were tangled together in a big knot like Mommy's necklaces. Sometimes they were so hard to fix that Mommy gave up and just let them stay like that forever. Would Emma feel like this forever too? Where would she sit at lunch without her Special Friend Crew? Lily would definitely not want to sit with her after the Big Spill this morning. And neither would Amelia; not after Lily told her what happened.

Ms. Smeltzer told the class to line up in backward alphabetical order. That meant Emma was at the end of the line. Last year, Mr. Cooper always had them line up in normal alphabetical order, never backward. Emma shuffled her feet behind Ben Brennan in his striped green shirt as they walked to the cafeteria. Ben was new at the end of last year. He didn't talk to other kids, and no one talked to him. He didn't smile. He wore shirts that buttoned all the way up and always tucked his shaggy hair behind his ears.

When they reached the cafeteria doors, Emma peered in. Without her regular table to sit at, the cafeteria looked like a giant pinball game. She would bounce around just like she did on the bus this morning. In the far corner, she saw Lily and Amelia sitting together already. They were whispering, their buns touching like a hair-high-five. It felt like someone was pinching Emma's heart.

Before she thought about what she was doing, she poked Ben in the back. He turned. He glared. Emma winced but she asked; she had no choice.

"Can I sit with you?".

"I sit alone." Ben sniffed and pushed his hair back.

"Why?" Emma asked.

Ben shrugged. "Kids talk and chew too loud." Emma took this in. If Ben thought all kids were too loud, how would he make any new friends at this school? Then she thought of Little's yelling and Big's chomping at the dinner table. Maybe Ben sat with boys like her brothers before. If so, she understood what he meant.

"I'll be quiet," Emma promised. Ben didn't answer. But he didn't say no. So Emma followed him through the cafeteria. He sat down at an empty table. Emma sat across from him.

Even though words were filling up her mouth and trying to burst out, Emma didn't let them. Otherwise, Ben would tell her to leave. She glanced at Lily and Amelia. Lily was moving her hands around. Amelia was laughing. Probably at Emma. Lily caught Emma looking at her. Emma opened and closed her mouth like she was talking, even though she had to stay quiet for Ben. Ben stared at her. Lily did too, then she said something to Amelia. Emma's ears were as hot as the worst sunburn ever. She looked down at her green lunch bag like it was her most interesting experiment yet. She took out the paper baggie inside and pulled out her sandwich. The bread was ruined, just like her snack. She thought back to that morning. Maybe instead of making a friendship potion she had mixed up a very-bad-day potion instead.

"What's that smell?" Ben asked, sniffing. Emma wished lunch would speed up; that the whole day would be over and she could climb into bed with her stuffed elephant, Emmaphant, and not ever come back to school again. Instead, she fastened the bag back up as quickly as she could. Now even Ben, who didn't have any friends, wouldn't like her.

"Is that vinegar?" he asked.

Emma moved her head in a half nod, half shake.

"Is that a yes or no?"

She moved her lips, mouthing the words, "It's partly vinegar."

"I can't hear you," Ben said.

She silently moved her mouth, "That's because you don't want me to talk."

"I know that smell because of a cool experiment I made," Ben said. Emma started to say something, then shut her mouth.

"Go ahead," he nodded.

"You do experiments?" Emma blurted out. Kids at the other tables turned. Emma put her hand over her mouth.

Ben nodded, "Yes, I have a very special book."

"Me too!" she said.

"Powerful Potions book?" they both asked at the same time. Emma's mouth dropped open.

"Yes. I use it all the time. My aunt gave it to me. It's the best book in the world," said Ben.

"It is! My Grandpa gave me mine." They grinned at each other. She'd never seen Ben's teeth before. He was like a different person now while smiling.

Emma said, "Hey, do you ever want to make some potions with me?"

"Okay," Ben said. He tucked his hair behind his ears.

Even though she didn't have a sandwich to eat, the rumbles in Emma's tummy didn't bother her for the rest of the lunch period. Ben even gave her his green apple, her favorite fruit. Ben liked just what she liked. He would be her new best friend and they would make billions of experiments together. She didn't need any friendship potions. And when Lily and Amelia heard about all the cool stuff she and Ben did together, they would wish it were them.

CHAPTER 5
The New Playdate Plan

The doorbell rang just as Emma finished setting out the Powerful Potions book. Next to it were her science kit, craft box, four measuring cups and a spoon for each, bowls of different sizes and colors, paper towels, two pairs of plastic gloves and two pairs of goggles. Everything was ready to go.

She ran to the door, Spiky right behind her, and swung it open.

"Hi Ben," she said.

Ben was already wearing a pair of science goggles and holding his own Powerful Potions book. He wore a white lab coat. His hair stuck up all around the headband. He pushed the goggles back on his nose, nodded at Emma and marched in the door.

Somehow, he knew where to find the kitchen. Emma scurried after him.

"Let's get started," he said, plunking his book down on top of hers.

"You didn't need to bring your own," Emma said.

"I did. I take notes on every experiment."

"Want to flip through for ideas?" Emma asked. She shifted back and forth. She didn't want to choose the wrong ones like she did with Lily and Amelia. Ben might say they were boring. Then she would feel Just Medium all over again. Ben turned right to a page in his book with the corner turned down.

"I already picked Galaxy in a Jar," he said. Emma thought about saying they should look at more choices and then pick together. But at the same time it was a really good experiment, the one she wanted to do the other day, the one Lily and Amelia said was boring.

"We'll need tempera paint, water, and glitter," said Ben.

"We have those. Also, cotton balls," Emma said, pulling the ingredients from her science boxes. Then they got to work, planning, measuring, pouring.

Galaxy in a Jar:

⅓ cup water.

Add a teaspoon of paint.

Stir.

Add cotton balls.

Add glitter.

Repeat.

The jar slowly transformed into a colorful, shimmering galaxy. Ben jotted down a note after every step.

Emma admired their creation. It was a great one. She looked at Ben. He was bent down low, his eye close to the jar. He straightened up and put his fingers together in a steeple. Emma held her breath. Did he like it? Then, he slowly nodded at Emma. She nodded back, a grin bursting through her lips.

They worked so well together. Maybe they'd go through the whole Powerful Potions book together in third grade.

"Should we do another one?" Emma asked.

"How about the anti-gravity version?" Emma didn't even know that one. Ben explained when you add baby oil and food coloring instead of paint to the mix the glitter travels up instead of down. Emma thought that was a cool idea. She couldn't stop smiling. Ben loved science as much as she did.

"Sperment time!" yelled Little as he ran into the room with Spiky at his heels. Ben winced and backed away.

"He loves to play with my friends," Emma explained.

"He might break something," Ben said.

Emma crouched down to Little. "You can help but only if you wait until I say so." Little kids weren't always good at being patient.

Little stood at the end of the table, gripping his

hands together and bouncing up and down as they worked on the anti-gravity Galaxy. Emma could tell it was hard for him to stay still. Spiky barked as Little bounced.

Ben made a shooing motion. "Don't you have a cage for him?" asked Ben.

Emma widened her eyes. "For Little?"

"No, for the dog."

"Oh. Come on, Spiky, time to go in your crate." She guided Spiky by his collar. She felt a little mean when she locked the crate door. But Ben was probably right. Spiky might get in the way.

When the jar got to the top, Little couldn't hold still anymore. He ran around the table.

"Okay, Little, it's your turn," Emma said. Ben sighed. Little took the jar delicately. He shook it carefully, his eyes growing bigger.

"Great job. Now just a little more so the colors blend," Emma instructed. Little shook harder. A lot harder.

The jar slipped out of Little's hands.

CRASH SPLASH

They all stared in silence at the exploded galaxy on the floor.

"Told you," said Ben.

Spiky started barking. Little started to cry.

"Don't worry, Little. It's like a supernova," Emma said, putting her hand on his shoulder.

"A supernova is when a star explodes, not a galaxy," Ben said.

Emma's stomach tightened. "I know that. I said it was 'like' one." Ben wrote a tiny note on the page. Emma tried to read it but it was too small. She wondered if it was about her.

Little's crying turned to wailing. He hid in his spot under the counter behind the stools. Emma's tummy felt ripped to shreds. Just then Mommy rushed in.

"Oh dear. Everyone watch out for the glass," she

said, motioning them out of the kitchen.

"He dropped the jar," Ben said, pointing at Little. Emma scrunched up her fists. She wanted to tell Ben that maybe he should be the quiet one this time. But then she would have even more changes to deal with.

"Okay, why don't you all clear out of here so I can sweep up?"

Little peeked out from his spot and Mommy led him to the couch next to Big. Ben grabbed his book and he and Emma retreated to the family room too. Little took in ragged gasps of air. Emma wanted to give him a hug. She held herself back. She didn't want to do another thing wrong and have another playdate fail. Even though it was probably too late.

"What's wrong, Little?" Big asked, putting his arm around his brother.

"Emma's friend doesn't like me," he said, pointing at Ben. Emma thought of how Lily invited Little to play with them and Amelia wrapped him up in a blanket.

"Want to come kick the soccer ball with us outside?" Big asked. Little jumped up and down, then ran out the door with Big and Spiky. Emma swallowed a big bubble in her throat as Big gave her a look over his shoulder.

"Should we go with them?" Emma asked.

"I don't play soccer," Ben said.

"It's just for fun. You don't need to really know how," Emma said.

"Nah."

"Legos?"

Ben shook his head.

"How about something different?" Emma suggested. She remembered the mistake she made on her last playdate. "I can try something new," she added, twisting her hands together.

"I came here for Powerful Potions. That was the plan," Ben said.

"I thought we were friends."

"We are. We're experiment friends."

"Like we're figuring it out?"

"No, like we are friends who do experiments. I think I'll call my mom now. This is getting boring." Emma's shoulders slumped. There it was again, that word: boring. Maybe Emma wasn't only just medium and naughty, but also just plain boring. Through the window, she saw the ball soar by. A soccer game with her brothers suddenly looked like the best game ever.

Ben wrote more notes in his book as he waited to be picked up. Emma kept silent just like she did at lunch with him the other day even though that wasn't going to help anymore. She covered her face with her hands. She didn't have her old best friends. She didn't have a new best friend. She didn't even have another plan. Instead, she had a whole new Friendship dil*Emma*.

CHAPTER 6
Big's Plans

"You're being weird," Big said to Emma as they climbed into the car the next day to drop Big at his friend's house. Then Emma and Dad were going to do errands together.

"Your feet smell like onions," Emma said back. If he was going to start a fight she was going to win.

"At it already?" Dad asked as he got into the front seat.

"I mean you're totally messing up all your playdates this week. The Powerful Pal Group was a disaster."

"It's Special Friend Crew!" Emma spat back.

"Whatever. And that guy Ben was making all the decisions, and he wasn't nice to Little, or even Spiky. And you let him. *Normal* you wouldn't let any of that happen. You should just be regular Emma Bemma."

"Don't tell me what to do."

Emma buckled her seatbelt. Then she buckled her arms over her chest to block Big's advice. He barely brushed his teeth and was obsessed with driving pretend video cars. What did he know?

The real car pulled out of the driveway. Emma looked out the window trying to ignore Big. Dad switched on the radio and hummed along to a terrible song from the olden days but she could still hear Big talking.

"Sometimes Jeremy's annoying. He throws things and squirms on the bus and bumps into me. But he's also cool because he'll play baseball when I want to, even though it's not his favorite."

"I'm not friends with Jeremy and I can't stand baseball."

"That's not the point. I…"

Emma interrupted. "Dad, can you turn up the music?" She didn't want to hear Big's advice anymore, even though something was clicking into place inside her mind, even if it was very hard to hear.

"Great song, huh? Glad you like it!" Dad said, twisting the dial up. He belted it out even louder. Emma stuck her tongue out at Big.

Big threw his hands in the air. "Fine. I'm just telling you. I'm in fifth grade. I've seen it all," he shouted.

A few minutes later, Dad pulled up to Jeremy's house. Big slammed the door when he got out. Dad looked at Emma in the rearview mirror.

"Good," Emma said.

"Good what?"

"Good, *he's* out of this car."

"You don't want your big brother's advice huh?"

"You could hear us?"

"Dads hear everything. I know you don't want your brother's unsolicited opinion, but he may have a point." He turned right out of Jeremy's driveway.

"What does that mean?"

"I'll translate Big language for you. What he was trying to say is that compromise is important. Communication too."

Emma was quiet for a moment. She let a bit of the advice sink in even though she wasn't sure she would keep it. She might throw it out the window and let all the cars run over it.

"Hey," Dad said, "Any interest in some ice cream?"

"Yes! Sundae?"

"How about a cone with sprinkles," Dad said, smiling in the mirror. "A compromise."

"Okay," said Emma. Compromise was sweet when it was ice cream.

CHAPTER 7
Little's Plan

That morning before school Emma tried to do her own hair for a long time, but it just wouldn't listen. She gathered it up, twisted it around, and tucked the strands in. Yet the hair band snapped at her skin, the pins she found in Mommy's drawer stabbed her head and her curls kept popping right out. Then she watched the video she'd found one more time and tried to transfer the ideas into her head. Emma did the best she could.

Before she went downstairs, Emma checked on her fish. Special was swimming in graceful circles in his bowl. Emma studied him for a minute. Then she nodded as she gave him a pinch of food. He knew her plan for the day. They always understood each other.

In the kitchen, Big sat at the counter chomping on cereal without milk like usual. When he saw Emma he spit a few pieces out. Gross.

"What's with the fancy 'do? Are you going to the ball?" he laughed. Emma scowled at him.

"None of your business," she said. She patted at her bun which was starting to unravel again.

Mommy was rummaging around in the container drawer. "Where's the one I put the lettuce in?" she asked herself.

A guilt bubble rose in Emma's throat as she remembered the container she left on the bus. It had been gone the next time she got on. Maybe it was in the lost and found by now. Maybe it wound up in someone else's kitchen container drawer.

Little and Spiky ran out from their hideout under the countertop. Little squatted next to Mommy, copying her motions.

"I'm Mommy," said Little, rearranging the drawer with her. "Where oh where is my Tuppaway?"

"Oh, well," Mommy sighed.

"Oh, well," Little echoed.

Mommy made turkey sandwiches for lunch. As she packed Emma's in a paper bag she shook her head and said, "Your green one stinks like vinegar." Emma pretended she didn't hear. She studied the white swirls on the green countertop like a world-class scientist.

"This is my new hat," Little announced. Emma looked up as he put a big container on his head. It covered his mouth.

"Nice look, dude," said Big, taking a scoop of cereal. He chewed with his mouth open. Ben would hate that.

"MMBMMM," Little gurgled from inside the plastic, as he ran around the kitchen island. Spiky joined the parade.

"Little, stop it. You're going to get hurt," Mommy said. Little took his hat off and put it on the floor. Then he pretended to pour invisible bottles into the container.

"I'm Emma Bemma." He stirred an imaginary spoon. "Mix, mix, mix it all up."

"Cool," Big commented, "are you making soup?"

"It's a secret potion," Little said. Emma's tummy tightened. She remembered him hiding under the counter that day. He knew about her best friend potion.

"Oooh, what kind?" asked Big.

"I can't tell you," Little said. He tiptoed to his

backpack and stuffed the container inside of it. Big stopped crunching as he watched. Emma felt herself turning red. He was going to get her in trouble.

"What's he talking about?" Mommy asked, cocking her head to the side.

"Emma's powafull potion," Little said.

Then he pulled the container out again and threw it in the air. He caught it, put it on the floor and sat in it.

"Ha, now it's a chair!" Big said.

"No! It's a potty!" said Little. Emma giggled. Now everyone would forget what he said about her. Little made everyone laugh even if they were upset.

Mommy shot Little a look. "You're too old for this."

"Sorry, Mommy. Everyone poops." He got off the potty and handed it back. She patted his head. Emma relaxed. Now Mommy would forget what Little said about Emma's secret. But then, Mommy turned to her and pulled Emma's eyes to hers like magnets.

"Em, is everything okay?" she asked. Her eyes roamed over Emma's bun. It was starting to give Emma a headache.

Emma nodded and sealed her lips. If she spoke, the whole story might come pouring out like the potion on the bus. Her eyes would be swollen and red for school, and she didn't want that, especially not with everyone looking at her like they would be today with her new idea. And this new idea was the final solution to the friendship mess.

Before she left for the bus, Mommy gave Emma an extra-tight hug. "I'm here when you're ready to talk," she said. Suddenly, Emma had a feeling Mommy knew much more than she thought. Parents were like that.

CHAPTER 8
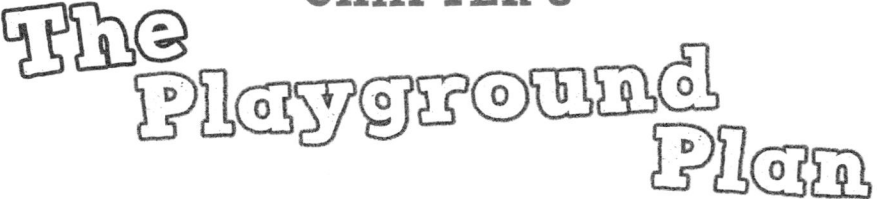
The Playground Plan

Ms. Smeltzer talked for five million years that morning. Emma tried to pay attention, but she couldn't stop looking out the window at the place where it was all going to happen. This was her last chance to make third grade a success. Otherwise, her family might have to move to China or Spain, and Emma wasn't even good at Spanish anymore.

A slapping sound made Emma turn and sit up straight. Ms. Smeltzer was handing back assignments. She tapped on the back of Emma's paper, "Your slice-of-life." Emma's stomach sank. Mr. Cooper gave out smiley-face stickers on second grade papers. Ms. Smeltzer probably gave out sad ones. Emma didn't need anything to remind her to frown about third grade. She needed to stay focused on recess. She slipped the paper into her desk without flipping it over.

* * *

It was finally time. Emma waited on the blacktop, the spot where the Special Friend Crew used to join up, right on top of the drawing of Connecticut. Soon Lily and Amelia walked out.

The girls walked towards her. Lily's mouth formed into an O. She was probably wondering why Emma was in their Special Friend Crew spot when the Special Friend Crew was broken in half, or really cracked in two-thirds and one other lonely third. She had to start before they got too close. Emma sparked into action. First, she raised up onto her toes. She made the kissing face Lily had made. She tiptoed around the playground with her arms held high just like in the video. Her toes felt like they might break. Still, she kept going, completing a tour around the whole map of the country. Then it was time for step

two. Emma began to twirl. Round and round she spun in a circle again and again, like an egg beater turning up the speed. The swings, the slide, the baseball field passed by, and soon, they were all a blur.

Once she couldn't turn anymore, Emma stopped. When she had planned this part, she didn't realize that the world would keep spinning without her. She tried to get her balance. She staggered a bit, and fell forward, catching herself with her hand. She felt a little bit nauseous. But the show had to go on. Wasn't that what Dad always said? Lily and Amelia's eyes were on her like she wanted. And lots of other people's eyes too. She couldn't stop now.

Emma backed up towards the swings. She took a deep breath and pictured what she'd seen in the video. Then she ran as fast as she could, faster than in any soccer game. She leapt up into the air when she reached the blacktop map. Her legs stretched in front of her. Time slowed down as she flew over the entire drawing of the country from Connecticut to Colorado to California. Maybe some people didn't even need ballet lessons and were naturally good at it. She soared through the air in slow motion. Lily and Amelia watched her with their mouths wide open. Emma smiled. This should have been her first plan.

Emma landed on one foot, ready to take a bow. Her ankle bent the wrong way and instead, she dove onto the blacktop.

Emma lay down in the Pacific Ocean. She rolled over and stared up at the sky so she didn't have to see everyone at recess laughing at her. A cloud dragon blew fire at her. She held her twisted ankle in one hand. Her final plan was a big flop.

"Are you okay?" Lily peered down at her. Emma closed her eyes.

"Should I call a teacher?" asked Amelia. Emma shook her head without opening her eyes. Her ankle ached. Her heart ached more.

"What *was* that?" asked Lily.

"A grand jetty," Emma whispered.

"You mean a grand jeté?" asked Amelia, saying the word all funny. Emma felt her face get red.

"I don't know. It was a ballet show."

"That was definitely *not* ballet," Amelia said. Emma pictured her shaking her head.

"But you don't even like ballet. Why would you even *do* that? And at recess?" asked Lily.

Emma sighed. She might as well tell them now that everything was ruined anyway. She would need to sit even farther away from them in the cafeteria. Maybe she could eat lunch in the hallway or in the classroom with Ms. Smeltzer and the turtle.

"I was doing it for you. But I messed up. Now we will never be the Special Friend Crew again." Emma's nose started to tickle. A salty drop trickled into her mouth.

"Emma," said Lily. Emma opened one eye. "You don't need to do ballet for us to be friends." Emma opened her other eye.

"But you two are still best friends and I... I'm all alone." Emma wiped a tear from her cheek.

"Why do you think we aren't friends anymore?"

"You didn't want to do Legos, or experiments or soccer and you weren't in row six on the bus, and..." Emma was out of breath. "I was trying to compromise. If I do ballet, we can stay friends."

"I wasn't in row six because someone took our spot. I was waiting for you, but then you spilled that stuff on me. What was that anyway?" Lily asked.

"A potion," Emma said softly. She looked away at the slide and wished she could hide under it like Little did under the countertop.

"We can't hear you," Amelia said.

"It was a best friend potion that didn't work," Emma said a little more loudly.

"Oh," said Lily, "That's a silly idea. Why didn't you tell me? I thought you didn't want to sit with me anymore. And it kind of seemed like you thought ballet was stupid." Lily bit her lip.

"It isn't stupid. I'm sorry," Emma said between sniffing.

"And I'm sorry you had to do a really weird dance in front of everyone and dive into the chalk ocean to try to be friends again," said Amelia.

"Yeah, I guess I'm not a very good ballerina." Emma laughed a little. It was nice. "And I'm definitely not good at buns." She pulled the hairband out of her hair and shook her head around. She felt lighter.

"We were always friends. We still are," said Lily.

"We are?"

"Definitely. We're still the Special Friend Crew," said Amelia.

Suddenly, Emma's ankle didn't hurt as much.

Lily's face brightened. "Hey! I have an idea for the weekend!" She held her finger up high above her head. Emma held her breath. She decided that whatever Lily said, she would give it a chance, even if it was a new idea. But the best part was that when

Lily shared her idea, Emma liked it a lot. She couldn't wait to tell Mommy.

The girls stayed and talked on top of the Pacific Ocean. It felt a little like last year, but also a little different. When the bell rang, Emma leaned on her friends as she hopped on one foot off the playground. Maybe the potion had worked after all.

CHAPTER 9
Sprained But Not Broken

Mommy held the door as Emma swung through on her new crutches into the house. Little ran after her. She plopped onto the couch and Mommy put some pillows under her foot. After the recess catastrophe, Mommy and Little had picked Emma up at the school nurse and taken her to the doctor. Emma told Mommy the whole story on the drive there, from playdate disaster to playground disaster. Now, even though her foot was all wrapped up like a mummy, she felt like she was floating.

The sound of clapping came from behind her. Emma twisted around to see Big applauding.

"What's that for?" she asked.

"I heard you were a hit at recess today." He snorted. "Were you trying out for *The Nutcracker*?"

"You heard that?"

"I'm twelve. I know a lot. And I *knew* something was up when I saw your hair nest this morning."

Emma's shoulders rose to her ears. "That was a ballet bun."

"Whatever you want to call it."

"Besides, I was taking *your* advice about compromise."

"Dude, when I told you about Jeremy, I didn't mean you should put on a performance in front of the whole school. But I sure wish I'd been in the audience." Big hooted and clapped some more. Then his gaze suddenly stopped at Emma's foot. His eyes widened.

"My grand jeté didn't end so well," Emma said.

"Does it hurt a lot?"

"Not too bad. It's just a sprain. It's not broken. Turns out the Special Friend Crew isn't broken either."

"Oh, good." Big looked relieved. He smiled. "Well, turns out I *haven't* actually seen it all." They both laughed.

Little ran in and picked up the crutches.

"Little, those are mine!" said Emma, but he was already zooming around the room. Spiky joined in the performance. He yipped, he barked, he jumped. He grabbed the end of a crutch and shook it around in his mouth. Little wrestled with him back and forth. Back and forth. They were definitely going to break the crutch. Finally, Little pulled one crutch free.

"Watch me," he then commanded. Turning in circles, Little went faster and faster. Spiky spun next to him, chasing his tail.

"I know! You're a ballerina," shouted Big over the noise.

"No, I'm Emma Bemma," Little yelled back.

"Little!" Emma cried, "That's not a good id…"

But it was too late.

CRASH

Down went Mommy's vase of flowers. Water splashed, glass crashed, pink petals scattered around the room. Mommy dashed over. Little's eyes got big.

"Mommy, look," he tried, pointing at the mess. "It's a star explosion." Mommy wasn't impressed at Little's supernova. She brought the curtain down on his show by telling him to march right to his room to think about his behavior. Emma squeezed Little's hand as he passed by, tears leaking down his face. She knew how it felt for your performance to end with a crash, even if it wasn't the best idea in the first place.

CHAPTER 10
Let's Start The Show

The next morning, Mommy popped into Emma's room.

"I have Ben on the phone. He has something to say to you." Emma took a deep breath and put Mommy's phone to her ear.

"Hello?"

"Hey, I apologize for my behavior at our playdate. I will com… comp." He seemed to be stuck on the word. "Compromise better in the future," he finished. It was like he was reading an essay aloud to the class. Emma thought about this for a minute. The script didn't sound like Ben, but it did sound familiar.

"Did your dad tell you to say that?" she finally asked.

Ben laughed. "My mom did."

"Oh." He was forced into it, she thought.

"But she was right," Ben said quickly. "It's just different at my house. I'm the only kid and my cat is really quiet and sleeps all day. The playdate wasn't exactly what I expected. I got upset. Sorry."

"I get it," Emma said. She really really did.

"You do?" He sounded relieved. He sounded more like Ben.

"Yup. But believe me, you don't want to hear my whole story. It's really long."

"Umm, do you want to be my partner in the science project next month?"

Emma wanted to jump up and down but that didn't work with crutches, so she bounced on her good foot's tiptoe.

"Yes," she said. The two of them talked about ideas. When Emma suggested they study pet fish, Ben agreed. Emma had a feeling it wasn't his first choice, but they were both learning how to compromise.

As soon as they hung up, Emma took a notebook and pencil over to her fish. It was time to start collecting data. At first, Special swam quickly to the right, while Star swam slowly to the left. Sunshine tread water, his blue fins fluttering back and forth. Then slowly they began to swim more in sync. It wasn't perfect, but that made it more interesting. Emma wrote it down. Then she took out a ruler to measure their water level. It was .2 inches lower than yesterday in Special's tank, .3 lower in Star's, and Sunshine's was almost exactly the same. Emma sprinkled food pellets into each of their bowls. They floated for a moment, then began to sink before the fish snapped them up. Emma jotted it all down.

Then she waved goodbye to her fish and zipped out the door on her crutches. She was getting good at them. And, she wanted to be right on time for her latest plan. This time it wasn't a secret one. It was a plan she made with her Special Friend Crew.

*** * * ***

The audience was buzzing. Emma and Mommy found a seat near the front. Suddenly, Amelia plopped down beside her. Her hair was long and straight again. She wore her favorite blue leggings.

"Aren't you supposed to be up on stage?" Emma asked.

"Actually, I found out ballet isn't for me. I like playing guitar more."

The lights went down. The curtains opened. The ballet recital began.

A stream of ballerinas glided onto the stage. Where was Lily? Emma craned her neck to see over the tall man in front of her. There she was, just right of center, her bun high and tight, her smile wide.

Lily flew. She twirled. She leapt. So *that* was a grand jeté. That was definitely not what Emma had done on the blacktop the other day.

She clapped for Lily until her hands hurt.

After the show, Emma and Amelia got to go backstage. Emma hugged Lily tight.

"You're a great ballerina," Emma said. Lily smiled wide, wider than she even did on stage.

"I'm happy you came," Lily said.

"Hey, you guys can come to my guitar recital too!" said Amelia. The girls agreed.

They talked about the show, how Lily had goosebumps beforehand, how the lights were so bright, and how a baby started crying in the middle of the last dance. Then they walked, and Emma crutched, outside together to wait for Emma's mom to take them back to her house for a playdate.

"So, what was in it?" Lily asked.

"In what?"

"The secret friend potion."

"It was a dash of green food coloring, a splash of vinegar, a sprinkle of… well, something extra special."

"What was that?" Amelia asked. Emma thought

of her three fish swimming around at home. How their water had been extra low the day of the secret friend potion. How a tiny bit of help from Special, Star, and Sunshine had brought the three friends back together.

"That's the part I'm going to keep a secret," Emma said.

"I have an idea," said Lily. She raised her finger up towards the sky. "Special friend crew move!"

The girls grinned at each other. They got in a circle. They clapped their hands together three times. Amelia and Lily jumped up while Emma went on tippytoe on her good foot to high-five all around. Lily's right hand whooshed through the air, missing Emma's. Was she going to hit Emma again? But then she stopped, shifted slightly, and changed direction. Their hands met, a little off-kilter but still together.

Emma thought about her slice-of-life paper. She didn't know yet if Ms. Smeltzer liked it or not. But no matter what it said, this slice of life was yummy. The best part was the happy ending, or really, the happy twist, because this slice-of-life story was definitely to be continued.

Andrea Chalon

ABOUT THE AUTHOR

Laura Wiltse Prior went from creating tales starring "Laura the Great" in her dad's studio office, to crafting short stories when she was supposed to be working in a business office, to writing books for kids in her very own office (well, one she shares with her son's Xbox). She loves reading anything and everything, sneaking cookie dough from the mixing bowl and playing tennis. When she isn't writing, Laura's ferrying her kids around, hiking with her dog Cody, or hanging with Casper the cat. She lives in Connecticut with her husband and three kids, the inspiration for her authentic family stories.